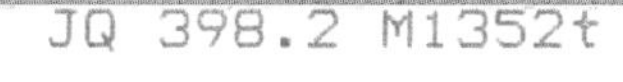
FEB 16 1997

Tuck-Me-In Tales

Bedtime Stories from Around the World

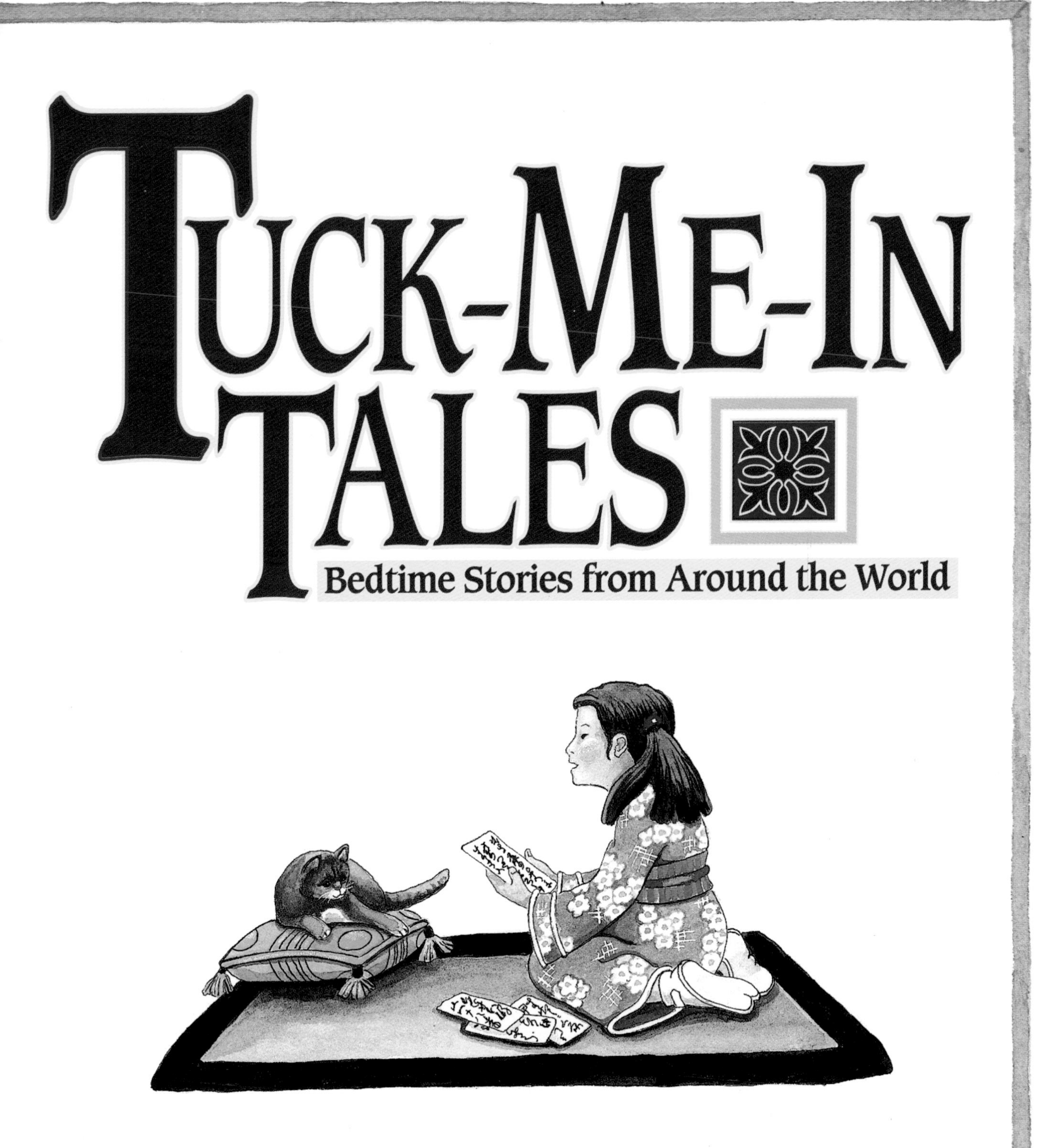

Margaret Read MacDonald

Illustrated by **Yvonne Davis**

AUGUST HOUSE

Little Folk

For all our grandchildren, now and to come
—MRM & YLD

For Colin, Evan & Kelsey
—YLD

Published 1996 by August House LittleFolk
P.O. Box 3223, Little Rock, Arkansas 72203
501-372-5450.

Book design by Harvill Ross Studios Ltd.

Manufactured in the United States.

10 9 8 7 6 5 4 3 2 1

LIBRARY OF CONGRESS CATALOGING-IN-PUBLICATION DATA

MacDonald, Margaret Read, 1940-
Tuck-me-in tales : bedtime stories from around the world /
Margaret Read MacDonald ; illustrated by Yvonne Davis.
p. cm.
Summary: Presents five folktales for young children, including "Snow Bunting's Lullaby" from Siberia, "Chin Chin Kobokama" from Japan, "Kanji-jo, the Nestlings" from Liberia, "The Playground of the Sun and Moon" from Argentina, and "Counting Sheep" from the British Isles.
ISBN 0-87483-461-9 (hc)
1. Tales. [1. Folklore.] I. Davis, Yvonne, ill. II. Title.
PZ8.1.M15924Tu 1996
398.2—dc20
[E] 95-53740

Many thanks to Bruce Carrick and The H.W. Wilson Company for permission to retell "The Snow Bunting's Lullaby" and "Kanji-jo, the Nestlings." Both appeared in slightly different form in Look Back and See: Twenty Lively Tales for Gentle Tellers *by Margaret Read MacDonald (Bronx, New York: H.W. Wilson, 1993).*

Thanks to Mariko Martin for critiquing the illustrations for "Chin Chin Kobokama."

The paper used in this publication meets the minimum requirements of the American National Standards for Information Sciences–permanence of Paper for Printed Library Materials, ANSI.48-1984

Contents

Snow Bunting's Lullaby

A Folktale from Siberia

In the spring, Mama and Papa Snow Bunting built a nest.
Mama laid a tiny egg.
She fluffed her feathers and sat on that egg.
Mama sat and sat and then . . .

"Peepeep!" Out came a little chick.

At once it began to cry.

"Peepeep . . . peepeep . . . peepeep . . ."

Mama Bunting said, "No no, don't cry. I'll sing you a lullaby." She spread her wings over the nest and sang:

"Go to sleep . . . go to sleep . . . go to sleep!"

The baby bird just kept on crying.

"Peepeep . . . peepeep . . . peepeep . . ."

"Let me try, Mama," said Papa Bunting.

Papa Bunting spread his wings over the nest.

He sang:

> "Whose little toes are these?
> Whose little wings are these?
> Whose little beak is this?
> Are . . . you . . . asleep?"

Sure enough, this lullaby put the chick to sleep.

"Ahmmmmm . . ."

"Thank you, Papa Bunting!" said Mama Bunting.
"I will sing that lovely song whenever our chick cries."

Papa Bunting flew off to find food for the family
and Mama Bunting settled down on the nest.
After a while the chick woke up and began to cry again.

"Peepeep . . . peepeep . . . peepeep . . ."

At once Mama began to sing Papa Bunting's lullaby.

"Whose little toes are these?
Whose little wings are these?
Whose little beak is this?
Are . . . you . . . asleep?"

It worked! The chick went back to sleep.

"Ahmmmmm . . ."

But there was Kutkha the Raven, flying past.
He was listening while Mama sang that lovely song.

"Mama Bunting, give me that song. I want to sing like that."

"Oh no, Kutkha. I must keep this song.
Papa Bunting gave it to me so I could put our baby to sleep."

"Well, if you won't *give* it to me," said Kutkha,
"I will just *take* it!"

The naughty Kutkha snatched the song right out of Mama Bunting's beak and flew off with it.
Baby Bunting woke up and began to cry.

"Peepeep . . . peepeep . . . peepeep . . ."

But Mama Bunting had no more song to sing.

Then Papa Bunting came home.

"Why aren't you singing, Mama?
Why is our baby crying?"

"Kutkha the Raven stole our song!
He snatched it right out of my beak and flew away with it!"

Papa Bunting's eyes flashed. He stamped his feet.

"We will see about *that*!
Bring my hunting gloves.
Bring my bow and arrows."

Papa Bunting set off running over the snow,
looking for Kutkha the Raven.
He spread his wings and began to fly,
over the mountains, down into a valley . . .

There was the raven colony.

Those ravens were all singing their raven song.

"Karr! Karr! Karr!"

Kutkha the Raven was sitting by himself,
singing the song he had stolen.

"Whose little toes are these?
Whose little wings are these?
Whose little beak is this?
Kutkha the Raven's! Huh! Huh! Huh!"

That Raven was laughing at his own joke.

“Kutkha the Raven!” called Papa Bunting.
“You give me back my song!”

“No, I won’t,” shouted Kutkha.

“I’ll keep it myself!”

"We will see about *that.*" Papa fitted a tiny arrow in his little bow.

Kutkha sang: "Whose little toes are these?"

Papa Bunting shot a tiny arrow right at Kutkha's toes.

"Oh. Oh! They're my toes! cried Kutkha.

But he went on singing:

"Whose little wings are these?"

Papa Bunting took aim again.

"Oh. Oh! They're *my* wings!"

Kutkha wouldn't stop:

"Whose little beak is this?"

Papa Bunting shot one more arrow.

"Oh. Oh! It's *my* beak! *Karr! Karr! Karr!*"

Kutkha coughed and dropped the song.

Papa ran swiftly and grabbed the song from the snow.

"Goodbye, Kutkha! If you want a lullaby,
you must make one up yourself!"

Papa flew straight back to Mama Bunting.

"Here, Mama. Now you can sing to our chick."

Mama Bunting spread her wings over the nest and sang.

"Whose little toes are these?
Whose little wings are these?
Whose little beak is this?
Are ... you ... asleep?"

"Ahmmmmm ..."

That baby was asleep.

CHIN CHIN KOBOKAMA
A FOLKTALE FROM JAPAN

When Mariko went to bed each night she cleaned her teeth with a tiny toothpick. But Mariko was too lazy to throw the toothpick away. She would just hide it under a corner of the tatami mat. She had been doing this for so long that there were hundreds of toothpicks under there.

One night Mariko was awakened by shrill little voices:

"Chin chin kobokama!"

On the floor of her room were hundreds of tiny samurai.
Each little warrior carried a sword.
They were charging each other and shouting:

"Chin chin kobokama!
Chin chin kobokama!"

In the morning Mariko was bleary-eyed.
She had not slept a wink all night long.

That night Mariko had just fallen asleep when . . .

"Chin chin kobokama!"

They were at it again.

Hundreds of tiny samurai . . . waving their swords and stabbing all around her room. Mariko sat as still as possible and watched them fight.

"Chin chin kobokama!
Chin chin kobokama!"

Mariko drew her feet up under herself and watched in alarm. She could not set one foot outside her bed for fear the little samurai would slice off her toes!

In the morning Mariko looked sleepier than ever. Her parents couldn't help but notice her sad state when she came to breakfast.

"Mariko, what on earth is wrong?
You look as if you haven't slept at all."

Poor Mariko broke down and began to weep.

"I don't think you will believe me, Father and Mother. Every night my room is overrun with tiny samurai warriors. They slice the air with their little swords and stab everything in sight. I dare not leave my bed for fear of being chopped!"

That night her father came to her room. He sat quietly in one corner with his sword drawn.

As soon as Mariko fell asleep, hundreds of tiny samurai began to crawl out from under the tatami mat. Each little man was dragging a tiny sword. They jumped up and began at once to duel.

> "Chin chin kobokama!
> Chin chin kobokama!"

Mariko's father watched all of this closely. He saw that each little sword was really nothing more than a toothpick!

In the morning her father questioned Mariko. “Do you have any idea where those little samurai are getting their toothpick swords?”

Slowly Mariko pulled back the tatami mat. There were hundreds of discarded toothpicks littering the floor.

Her father explained that the tiny samurai were drawn to her room because she provided so many excellent swords for their practice!

Mariko spent the day cleaning her room. She picked up every toothpick. She cleaned out every crack in those floorboards. She swept and swept and swept until her room was very clean.

That night she slept well at last.

And since Mariko never littered her room again, the little samurai did not return.

Kanji-jo, the Nestlings

A Mende Folktale from Liberia

On the banks of the Kanji River a mother bird laid five eggs.
For a long time she sat on those eggs.
She spread her feathers over them and kept them warm.

Now and then she would sing to the eggs.

"I laid five eggs long ago
by the Kanji River-o ...
I laid five eggs long ago ..."

Then she would stand and fluff her feathers.

"Kanji-jo, gebeti-jo,
kanji-jo, gebeti-jo."

Just as the chicks were about to pop from their eggs,
a hunter caught the mother bird and carried her off.

She soon managed to escape from his bag,
but by that time she was far from her nest.

Meanwhile the sun shone so warmly on the eggs
that they began to hatch.

The first egg rolled over.

Peck . . . peck . . . peck . . .

Out came a baby bird.

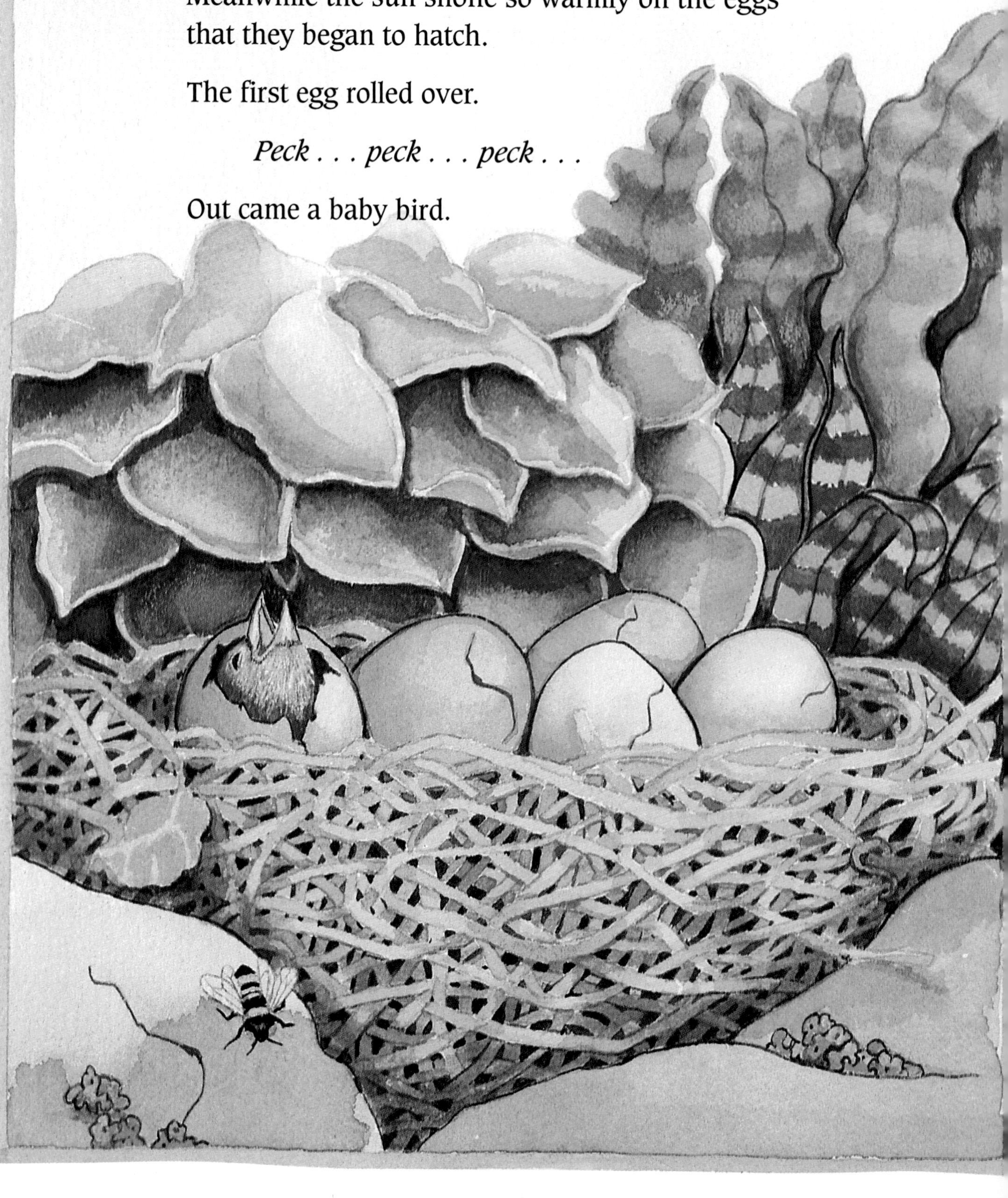

The second egg began to move.

Peck . . . peck . . . peck . . .

Out popped another.

The third egg: *Peck . . . peck . . . peck . . .*

The fourth: *Peck . . . peck . . . peck . . .*

The fifth: *Peck . . . peck . . . PECK!*

There were five baby birds in the nest.

They began at once to cry for their mother.

"Ma-ma! Ma-ma! Ma-ma!"

But there was no mother in sight.

"Our mother has gone!
We must look for our mother!"

The little birds climbed down from their nest.
They began wobbling down the road on their weak little legs.

"Ma-ma! Ma-ma! Ma-ma!"

There was Mrs. Bushfowl.

"Ma-ma! Ma-ma! Ma-ma!"

They clustered around Mrs. Bushfowl.

"Oh dear, are these *my* children?" said Mrs. Bushfowl.
"I didn't know I had five children.
But they are calling me 'Ma-ma' so they must be mine."

She took the little chicks into her nest.
She fed them their supper and put them to bed for the night.

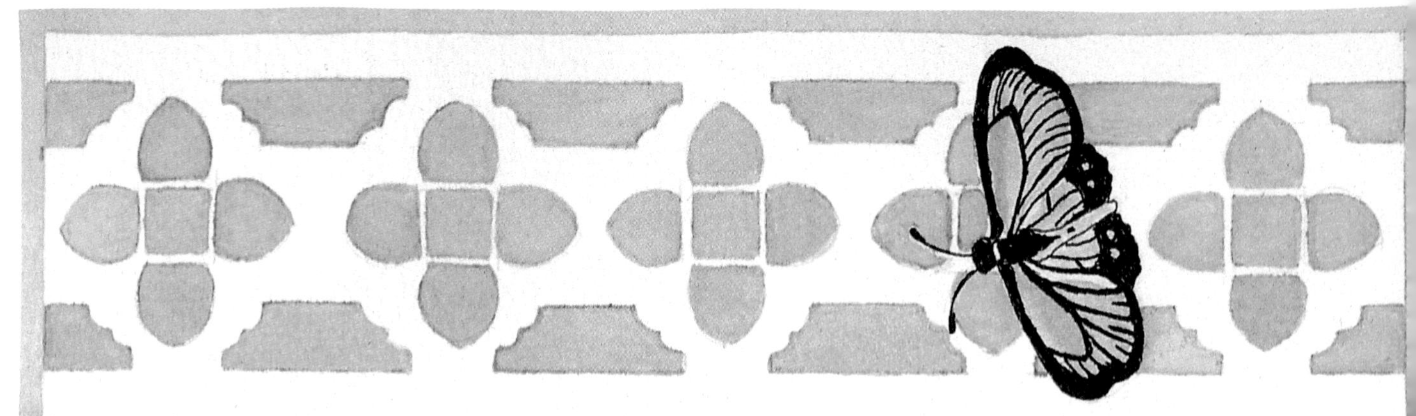

In the morning the five little birds looked at their new mother.
She was big and brown and fluffy.
They were small, and their feathers seemed to be blue.

"Pardon us, but are you really our mother?
Our mother sang a beautiful song when we were in our eggs.
Would you sing your song so we will know you are our mother?"

Mrs. Bushfowl ruffled her feathers.
She began to sing. "Ko-ko-yé! Ko-ko-yé! Ko-ko-yé!"

"*That's* not our mother's song. *This* is our mother's song:

> I laid five eggs long ago
> by the Kanji River-o . . .
> I laid five eggs long ago . . .
> Kanji-jo, gebeti-jo,
> kanji-jo, gebeti-jo."

"That's a lovely song," said Mrs. Bushfowl.
"But I can't sing like that.
I must not be your mother.
You'd better go look for her."

So the little birds went on down the road.
They were feeling stronger now.
They marched along calling: "Ma-ma! Ma-ma! Ma-ma!"

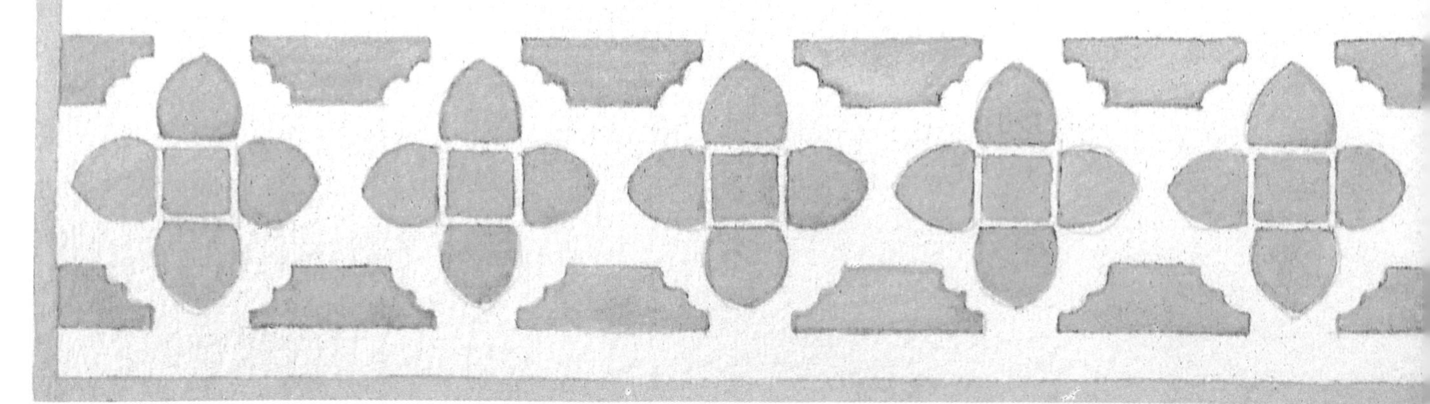

In the evening they met Mrs. Dove.

"Ma-ma! Ma-ma! Ma-ma!"

"Oh, are these *my* children?" said Mrs. Dove.
"I didn't know I had five children.
But they are calling me 'Ma-ma!'
They must be mine."

She took them into her nest.
She fed them their supper and put them to bed.

In the morning the five little chicks looked at their new mother.
She was shaped in a special dove way.
She seemed not like them at all.

"Pardon us, but are you really our mother?
Our mother sang a beautiful song when we were in our eggs.
Would you sing your song so we will know you are our mother?"

Mrs. Dove stretched her graceful neck and began to sing.

"Coo-oooooo . . . cooo-ooooo . . . coo-ooooo . . ."

"*That*'s not our mother's song. *This* is our mother's song:

I laid five eggs long ago
by the Kanji River-o . . .
I laid five eggs long ago . . .
Kanji-jo, gebeti-jo,
kanji-jo, gebeti-jo!"

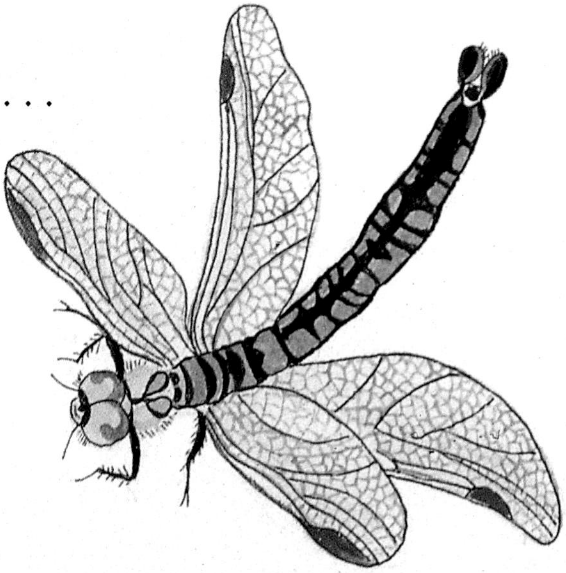

“That *is* a lovely song,” said Mrs. Dove.
“I can’t sing like that. I am certainly not your mother.
You must go and look for her.”

So the little birds rushed off.

“Ma-ma! Ma-ma! Ma-ma!”

In the evening they met Mrs. Sunbird.

"Ma-ma! Ma-ma! Ma-ma!"

"Oh my, these big babies are calling me 'Ma-ma'!
I didn't know I had five children. And so *large*!
Well, come into my nest and I'll give you your dinner."

In the morning the five little birds looked at their new mother.
She was nearly as small as they were.

"Can this really be our mother?
Our mother sang a beautiful song when we were in our eggs.
Sing your song, so we will know you are our mother."

Mrs. Sunbird began to buzz around the nest making her song:

"*Kawunggg . . . kawunggg . . . kawunggg . . .*"

"*That's* not our mother's song. *This* is our mother's song:

I laid five eggs long ago
by the Kanji River-o . . .
I laid five eggs long ago . . .
Kanji-jo, gebeti-jo,
kanji-jo, gebeti-jo."

"What a lovely song! I can't sing like that.
I must not be your mother."

So the little birds went on their way.

"Ma-ma! Ma-ma! Ma-ma!"

Meanwhile, their mother had escaped from the hunter.
She flew back to her home, but the nest was empty.
She hurried down the road looking for her chicks.
"Mrs. Bushfowl! Have you seen my children?"
"Where there five of them?" Mrs. Bushfowl replied.
"Yes!"
"Did they sing a lovely song?"
"I expect they did."
"They went right down this road."

“Mrs. Dove! Mrs. Sunbird! Have you seen my children?”

“Were there five of them?” Mrs. Dove answered.

“Yes.”

“Were they singing a beautiful song?” Mrs. Sunbird asked.

“I think they were.”

“They went right down this road.”

The mother bird ran after her children.

"Chick . . . chick . . . chick . . . chick . . . chick . . ."

The chicks heard her calling.
They turned and looked.
This mother had blue feathers like theirs, only more brilliant!
This mother was shaped just like them, only bigger!
She was just the right size to be their mother!

The five little chicks *ran* to that mother bird.

"Ma-ma! Ma-ma! Ma-ma! Ma-ma! Ma-ma!"

"Chick! Chick! Chick! Chick! Chick!"

They hugged one another.
They ruffled one another's feathers.

Mother Bird made a nest for her babies.
She fed them. She put them to bed for the night.

"Sing us your song!
Sing us your song, so we will know you are our mother!"

"Wait," said Mother Bird.
"In the morning we will sing.
In the morning we will dance.
In the morning I will teach you how to fly."

In the morning Mother Bird woke first of all.
She bent her head over the nest
and looked at her sleeping children.
Then she began to sing.

> "I laid five eggs long ago
> by the Kanji River-o . . .
> I laid five eggs long ago . . ."

When the little birds heard that, they jumped to their feet. They began to flap their wings and dance!

"Kanji-jo, gebeti-jo!"

This really was their mother.

All day long they danced and sang.

"Kanji-jo, gebeti-jo!
kanji-jo, gebeti-jo!
kanji-jo, gebeti-jo!"

And then, in the cool of the evening,
they spread their wings and flew.

"Kanji-joooooo . . .
kanji-joooooo . . .
kanji-joooooo . . ."

The Playground

An Araucanian Folkt

Some people say that high in the sky,
the sun lives in a palace of gold.
Sun looks out his window each morning
to see if Moon is in sight.

> "Where are you, little Moon?
> Are you hiding in the nighttime fields?
> Or are you playing in my blue day skies?"

om Chile and Argentina

Sometimes Moon is nearby, drifting pale in the bright daytime. She answers sweetly: "Did you call me, Sun?"

"Sure I called you!" Sun shoots his rays toward her.

"What do you want to play today?" asks Moon shyly.

"Ring of Fortune!" That is what Sun calls his game of chase.

"Oh? And how is it played?"

Then Sun begins to chant the directions:

"I have two rings
that are two paths.
One is day,
the other, night.
Tell me, Moon,
Which do you take?
The gold is day,
the silver, night."

Moon never hesitates at all.

"Me? I take the night!"

Then Sun jumps up, laughing.

"Then run, run, run!
And if I catch you,
I get your silver ring!"

So Moon dances off through the blue sky
and Sun runs happily after.

Of course Sun never catches Moon.
Moon crosses the sky and slips away
into her lovely fields of darkness.

There she dances and sings all night long,
drifting gently among the shadows.

Watch the sky and you will see . . .
there goes Moon in the daytime sky,
with Sun trailing behind.

But never will you see Sun move
within the nighttime sky.
The night belongs to Moon and Moon alone.

Counting Sheep

An Endless Tale from the British Isles

There once was a little shepherdess who cared for a large flock of sheep. Since it was springtime there were many momma sheep. And each momma sheep had a little baby lamb.

Every morning the little shepherdess would take her sheep to pasture. Every evening she would bring them home again. On the way home, those sheep had to jump over a little stone fence.

Here comes the first momma sheep to jump the fence.

"Baaa . . . baaa . . ."

Here comes her little lamb: "Baaa . . ."

Here comes the second momma sheep to jump the fence.

"Baaa . . . baaa . . ."

Here comes her little lamb: "Baaa . . ."

Here comes the third momma sheep to jump the fence.

"Baaa . . . baaa . . ."

Here comes her little lamb: "Baaa . . ."

Here comes the fourth momma sheep to jump the fence . . .

Telling These Stories to Children

We hope you will read these stories aloud many times, so often that you begin telling them without the book. In sharing "Snow Bunting's Lullaby" and the nestlings' "Kanji-jo" song you could use the tunes I suggest or just make up your own. My sources do not tell us what tunes the original tellers sang, so I had to invent my own. So, like Papa Bunting, you may want to do the same!

Snow Bunting's Lullaby

This story has a soft, gentle feel. I tend to downplay the bit of violence in which Papa Bunting attacks Raven, whom I depict as sassy and unruly rather than scary. The entire story, in fact, plays much like a lullaby. If telling to one or two children, I touch each one gently on their toes, "wings," and "beak" as I sing, as if trying to lull them to sleep. Even when telling this story to a large group of children I retain this feeling of singing them all to sleep during the story's lullabies.

Chin Chin Kobokama

This is a lively little teaching tale. The children will want to chant "Chin chin kobokama!" with you, especially when hearing the story for a second or third time. For daytime use, in story hour or in the classroom, the story can be quite active; I make little stabbing motions and chant vigorously with the samurai. For bedtime, of course, I subdue the motions and the vigor of my chanting.

Your children may want to look for the many folk toys depicted throughout this story: daruma (red papier-mache tumbler); hime daruma (princess daruma); sankaku daruma (pointy-headed daruma); inu hariko (papier-mache dog); usagi (white moon-shaped hare); long-nosed tengu (wooden doll); bullfinch of Kameido (perched wooden bird); Ise kami-dori (divine birds of Ise, carved wood); saru (carved monkey in pointed hat); usagi-garuma (rabbit on wheels); red-bird garuma (wooden wheeled toy); zyori-ningyo (puppet doll); nara ningyo (carved wooden Noh actor); hakata-ningyo (painted clay male doll); anesama ningyo (folded-paper doll); momotaro (folktale boy in wooden peach); Fugu-bue (clay blowfish whistle); and a cricket cage.

(In Japan, a child paints in one eye of a daruma doll and makes a wish. If the wish is granted, the second eye is added.)

Kanji-jo, the Nestlings

When reading this story at bedtime, you will want to keep the nestlings' singing soft and gentle. At the end they fly away with a soft "kanji-joooo." You may want to cuddle your children close and rock as you sing. When sharing this story with a group of children during the day, however, a more active telling is fun. I encourage the children to flap their wings and pretend to dance every time the nestlings chant, and at the end they often spread their wings and soar.

This story is great fun to dramatize as well. I usually choose a few children (or parents) to act the parts of the mother birds. I gather the rest of the children into a group to be the baby chicks (the number in the text can be adjusted to the number of "chicks" you have that day). We troop from mother bird to mother bird dancing our chant. I tell the story as we go, providing whatever dialogue I need to if my "actors" are too young or too shy. Older children, of course, will soon take over the story and make it their own.

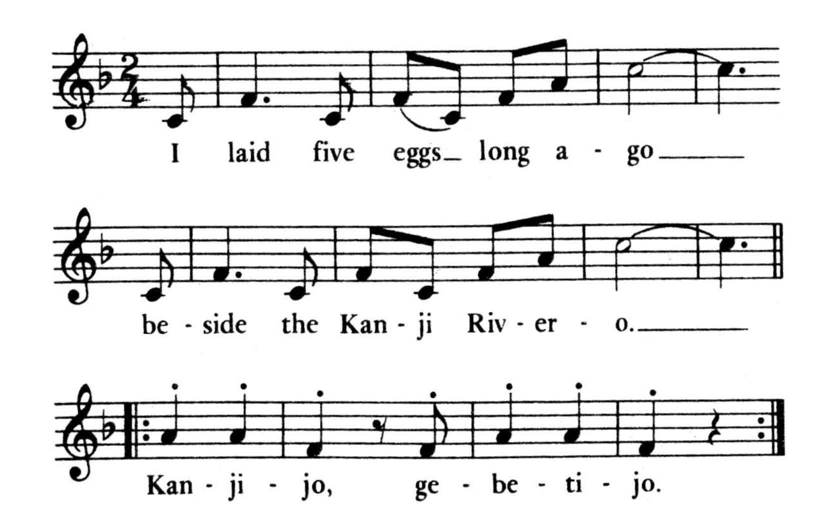

The Playground of the Sun and Moon

This story should be related in a gentle, magical tone. As a bedtime story, it has a lullaby quality to it. I especially like the reassuring notion of the night as a dark time that the moon *chooses* for its loveliness. For classroom use, this story makes a nice little playlet and can be performed with paper plate masks or large Sun and Moon masks of construction paper or papier-mache. The "rings" can be shown as rings for the finger in a bedtime setting or as much larger hoops in a dramatization.

Counting Sheep

The last story in this collection draws on a useful folk motif employed around the world to put children to sleep—or to end a storytelling session. The teller begins as if telling a complete story, then repeats ... and repeats ... and repeats, in hopes that smaller children will fade away into sleep. (And older children, seeing the futility of waiting for more stories at this point, often close their eyes and begin to drift away as well!)

About the Stories

Snow Bunting's Lullaby is told to children in Siberia. There the snow bunting is one of the first birds to return each spring to build its nest. The illustrations depict snow bunting *(plectrophenax nivalis)* and raven *(corvus corax)*. Variants of this story may be found in *Kutkha the Raven: Animal Stories of the North* translated by Fainna Solaska (Moscow: Malysh Publishers, 1981) and in *Life with Granny Kandiki: Based on Tales from the Soviet North* by Anna Garf (Moscow: Progress Publishers, 1978). Neither source states exactly which Siberian culture tells this story, but the illustrations for both books show Chuckchi clothing. Related folktale motifs: *A2245.1 Thrush steals woodcock's song; G555.1.1. Sing or I'll eat you. Ogre threatens; D1962.4.2 Song used to lull children to sleep.*

Chin Chin Kobokama was once a favorite of children in Japan. Lafcadio Hearn retold a variant of this in his *Japanese Fairy Tales* (New York: Liveright, 1953) and a retelling is found in Florence Sakade, *Japanese Children's Favorite Stories* (Rutland, Vermont: Tuttle, 1958). Related folktale motifs: *Q321 Laziness punished.*

Kanji-jo, the Nestlings is told to children by the Mende people of West Africa. We were lucky to find versions by four different Mende storytellers, so this tale combines bits from several tellers. Among the four versions we found reference to nine different birds. For this retelling we chose to depict bushfowl *(francolinus swainsonii)*, laughing dove *(streptopelia senegalensis)*, and the malachite sunbird *(nectarina famosa)*. In no variant is the species of the nestlings named, so we selected the colorful lilac-breasted roller *(coracias caudata)*.

Variants of this story may be found in *Royal Antelope and Spider: West African Mende Tales* by Marion Kilson (Cambridge, Massachusetts: Press of Langdon Associates, 1976) and in *Defiant Maids and Stubborn Farmers: Tradition and Invention in Mende Story Performance* by Donald Consentino (Cambridge, England: Cambridge University Press, 1982). The chant is from a version of the tale collected by Kilson from a man from Bumpe in Bo, April, 1960. Related folktale motifs: *Z30 Chains involving a single scene or event without interdependence among the individual actors.*

The Playground of the Sun and Moon was once told to Araucanian children in the southernmost tip of Chile and Argentina. This story is elaborated from an episode in "Cuando el Sol y la Luna Olvidaron la Tierra: cuento basado en una leyenda mapuche-ranculche" by Alicia Morel in *Cuentos Aruacanos: Le Gente de la Tierra* (Santiago: Editorial Andres Belloe, 1982). Her tales were derived from *Diccionario Comentado Mapuche-Espanol* by Esteban Erize (Buenos Aires: Instituto de Humanidade, Universidad Nacional del Sur, 1960). The tale from which it is extracted was collected by Lehman Nietshe from a Ranculche teller in southern Argentina. Related folktale motifs: *A722.9 At dawn sun comes to play with the moon; A735 Pursuit of sun by moon.*

Counting Sheep is an adaptation of Stith Thompson motif *Z11 Endless tales. Hundreds of sheep to be carried over river one at a time, etc.*